"Practice makes perfect!" It is through practice that children gain self-confidence and proficiency in their reading and writing skills. And parents can help. The stories and activities in **Hello Reader! Hello Writer!** books enable a parent to support and enhance the reading and writing strategies that are taught in school.

The stories in **Hello Reader! Hello Writer!** books are written with familiar words and short sentences that emerging readers can handle. Games and activities provide practice with skills such as word building, sentence building, grammar, reading comprehension, listening comprehension, following directions, and handwriting and letter formation. Best of all, the stories are fun to read, and the activities are fun to do!

So enjoy the story! Enjoy the activities! And most of all, enjoy your new reader!

Strategies for Sounding Out New Words

If your child comes to a word he or she doesn't know, encourage him or her to try one of these techniques:
- Say the beginning sound.
- Try the vowel sound. (Skip the vowel if it's too hard.)
- Say the ending sound.
- Blend the sounds together.
- Think of another word that looks like this word or rhymes with it.
- Look for familiar word parts or syllables.
- Talk to your brain: What word fits in the sentence? What makes sense?
- Look for picture clues.

About the Activities

The activities in this book are designed to enhance and accelerate learning. They are not meant to be done in one sitting. You should take your cues from your child. Some children enjoy paper and pencil tasks and written reinforcement. Other children try to avoid any written tasks.

You can encourage, reinforce, and prompt. But time spent together should be fun and stress-free. If your child becomes tired, put the book away for another time.

On most pages, you will need to read the instructions to your child.

To Megan
—G.M.

To the beginning readers and writers at
Laurel Plains Elementary School
—A.P.

For Jimmy
—L.F.

ISBN 0-439-33017-3

Text copyright © 2002 by Grace Maccarone.
Literacy activities copyright © 2002 by Alayne Pick.
Illustrations copyright © 2002 by Laura Freeman.
All rights reserved. Published by Scholastic Inc.
SCHOLASTIC, HELLO READER, CARTWHEEL BOOKS, and associated logos are trademarks and/or registered trademarks of Scholastic Inc.

10 9 8 7 6 5 4 3 2 1

02 03 04 05 06

Printed in the U.S.A.
First printing, January 2002

The 100th Day

Story by Grace Maccarone
Literacy Activities by Alayne Pick
Illustrated by Laura Freeman

Hello Reader! Hello Writer!
Level 1

Cartwheel
·B·O·O·K·S·®

SCHOLASTIC INC.
New York   Toronto   London   Auckland   Sydney
Mexico City   New Delhi   Hong Kong

Today is the 100th day of school
in Miss Hill's class.

Jill likes to make things.
She uses 100 beads
to make four necklaces.
Each necklace has 25 beads.

Jack does not want
to make necklaces.

Ben likes to write stories.

He writes about 100 cats.

20 are black.

20 are orange.

20 are white.

20 are gray.

20 have stripes.

Jack does not want
to write a story.

Kate likes to draw.

She draws 100 stars.
50 are silver.
50 are gold.

Jack does not want
to draw.
What will Jack do?

Jack looks out the window.

He wants to run.

He wants to jump.

Jack has an idea.

He will jump to 100.

Can he do it?

Jill gets the rope.

She and Ben turn it.

Everyone counts together

as Jack jumps.

1 2 3 4 5 6
7 8 9 10 11 12 13
14 15 16 17 18 19 20
21 22 23 24 25
26 27 28 29
30 31 32 33 34
35 36 37 38 39
40 41 42 43 44 45
46 47 48 49 50

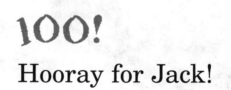

100!
Hooray for Jack!

WORD LIST

a	everyone	Kate	stripes
about	for	likes	the
an	four	looks	things
and	gets	make	to
are	gold	Miss	today
as	gray	necklace	together
beads	has	necklaces	turn
Ben	have	not	uses
black	he	of	want
can	Hill's	orange	wants
cats	hooray	out	what
class	idea	rope	white
counts	in	run	will
day	is	school	window
do	it	she	write
does	Jack	silver	writes
draw	Jill	stars	
draws	jump	stories	
each	jumps	story	

Ben likes to write about cats.

Color 20 cats black.

Color 20 cats orange.

Color 20 cats gray.

Color 20 cats with stripes.

Leave 20 cats white.

Make-a-Word

- Cut out the letters **r**, **t**, **s**, **w**, **e**, and **i**.
- Starting at the green dot, put the word **it** in the word tray.
- Add a letter to spell **wit**. (You will have to shift two letters to the right.)
- Change one letter to spell **sit**.
- Change the last letter to spell **sir**.
- Add a **silent e** to the end to spell **sire**.
- Change the beginning sound to spell **wire**.
- Change the beginning sound again to spell **tire**.
- Change the letter order around to spell **rite**.
- Listen for the beginning, middle, and ending sounds. See the **silent e**!
- Add the letter **w** to the beginning of the word. (You will have to shift four letters to the right.) **W** is silent.

- Now add the last letter **s** to the end of the word. What does the word say? It says **writes**.
- Study the word with your eyes. Now scramble the letters.
- Respell the word with the letters.
- Scramble the letters and spell the word again. Write the word from memory. If spelling the word from memory is too hard, match the word from print.

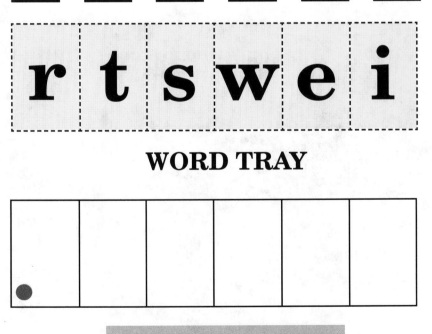

WORD TRAY

Skill: Word Building

Punctuation Pointers

What will Jack do?

He will jump to 100.

Read the two sentences above.
Each sentence has a different
punctuation mark at the end.
Find the two punctuation marks.

One is a question mark (?).

It shows that the sentence is asking a question.

With your right finger, point to the question mark.

Read the question.

Now find the period.

A period ends a statement.

A statement tells what happened.

Read the sentence with the period at the end.

Every sentence or question starts with a capital letter.

Point to the capital letters at the beginning of each sentence on the top of the page.

Now put the correct punctuation at the end of these sentences.

Add a question mark or a period.

Jack will jump to 100

Can he do it

Sentence Cut-Ups

Use scissors to cut apart the sentence
in the pink box below.

Leave all punctuation attached to the
closest word.

Scramble the words.

Unscramble the words to remake
the sentence.

Use punctuation as clues:

th, as in 100th, is the way you show
number order

' or **'s** shows that something belongs
to someone (Miss Hill has a class. It is
Miss Hill's class.)

. shows the end of a sentence

CAPITAL LETTERS show the beginning of
the sentence or someone's name.

Play it again!

Today	is	the	100th	day	of

school	in	Miss	Hill's	class.

Today is the 100 th day of school in Miss Hill's class.

Make it harder!

Cut apart the punctuation.

Cut off the **th**.

Cut off the apostrophe (') and the **s**.

Cut off the **period** (.).

Remake the sentence.

Play it again!

Sound Boxes

To the parent: Dictate these words in the following order: **run, gold, things**. Have your child listen for each sound and write each sound in a sound box. (The **th** is one speech sound. Therefore both letters are written in one box). If your child does not know the vowel sound, write it in the box for him or her. Instruct your child to start at the box with the green dot.

Write the word you just heard.

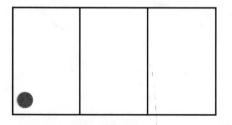

Write the word you just heard.

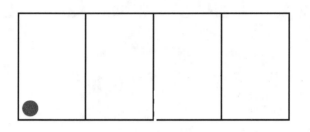

Write the word you just heard.
Remember to keep the **th** in one box.
It makes one sound.

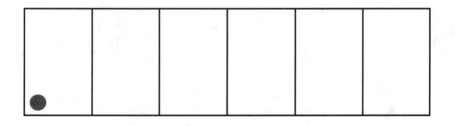

Happy Handwriting

Use the chart above to help you copy the sentence at the top of the next page. Leave a space as wide as your finger between each word.

_____ likes

to write.

_____

- -

_____

_____

- -

_____

To the parent: Have your child use a thick pencil. Grippers that are placed over regular pencils can be very helpful to new writers.

As your child copies the sentence, pay close attention to his or her letter formation. All circles should be formed from the top down—not from the bottom up. To cue your child to the proper circle letter formation, have him or her hold his or her left hand in a semi-circle. The forefinger is the correct starting place; the pencil moves counter-clockwise.

Skill: Letter Formation

Really Writing

Use the words **run, gold,** and **things** in a sentence.

Remember:
- Begin the sentence with a capital letter.
- Use capital letters with all names and the word **I**.
- Use a finger space between each word.
- End the sentence with a period.

_____

_____

_____

_____

To the parent: If your child has trouble creating a new sentence, you can dictate this sentence: "Jill will run and get the gold things in the box."

Skill: Sentence Writing